P9-COP-790

BOSTON
Tea Party

BOSTON
Tea Party

by PAMELA DUNCAN EDWARDS

illustrations by HENRY COLE

G. P. Putnam's Sons / New York

Text copyright © 2001 by Pamela Duncan Edwards.
Illustrations copyright © 2001 by Henry Cole. All rights reserved.
This book, or parts thereof, may not be reproduced in any form
without permission in writing from the publisher. G. P. Putnam's Sons,
a division of Penguin Putnam Books for Young Readers,
345 Hudson Street, New York, NY 10014. G. P. Putnam's Sons,
Reg. U.S. Pat. & Tm. Off. Published simultaneously in Canada.
Printed in Hong Kong by South China Printing Co. (1988) Ltd.
Book designed by Gunta Alexander. Text set in Ellington.
The art was done in acrylic paints and colored pencils on
Arches Hot Press watercolor paper.
Library of Congress Cataloging-in-Publication Data
Edwards, Pamela Duncan.
Boston Tea Party / by Pamela Duncan Edwards ; illustration by Henry Cole.
p.   cm.   1. Boston Tea Party, 1773—Juvenile literature.
[1. Boston Tea Party, 1773. 2. United States—History—Revolution,
1775–1783—Causes.] I. Cole, Henry, 1955–   ill. II. Title.
F215.7 .E36 2001   973.3'115—dc21   00-040270
ISBN 0-399-23357-1   10 9 8 7 6 5 4 3 2 1
First Impression

To Janie West, a devoted teacher — P. D. E.

For Roberta, my cup of tea! With love — Hen

These are the leaves that grew on a bush in a far-off land and became part of the Boston Tea Party.

This is the tea that was made from the leaves
that grew on a bush in a far-off land
and became part of the Boston Tea Party.

This is the king on his English throne
who declared, "Tax the tea!"
that was made from the leaves
that grew on a bush in a far-off land
and became part of the Boston Tea Party.

These are the colonists who cried, "No!"
to the king on his English throne who declared,
"Tax the tea!" that was made from the leaves
that grew on a bush in a far-off land
and became part of the Boston Tea Party.

This is the cargo being carried in ships to the shores
of the colonists who cried, "No!"
to the king on his English throne who declared,
"Tax the tea!" that was made from the leaves
that grew on a bush in a far-off land
and became part of the Boston Tea Party.

Look! The *Dartmouth*, the *Eleanor* and the *Beaver* are about to set sail.

They're going to Boston.

With tea from the British East India Company.

These are the patriots who made plans to dump the cargo
being carried in ships to the shores
of the colonists who cried, "No!"
to the king on his English throne who declared,
"Tax the tea!" that was made from the leaves
that grew on a bush in a far-off land
and became part of the Boston Tea Party.

These are the disguises worn by the patriots
who made plans to dump the cargo
being carried in ships to the shores
of the colonists who cried, "No!"
to the king on his English throne who declared,
"Tax the tea!" that was made from the leaves
that grew on a bush in a far-off land
and became part of the Boston Tea Party.

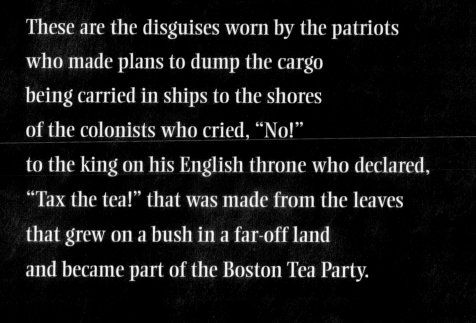

Dressing up as Mohawks
will fool the British!

We'll sneak on board
and surprise the sailors.

Make sure you don't
dump any cheese
by mistake!

These are the sailors scared by disguises worn by the patriots
who made plans to dump the cargo
being carried in ships to the shores
of the colonists who cried, "No!"
to the king on his English throne who declared,
"Tax the tea!" that was made from the leaves
that grew on a bush in a far-off land
and became part of the Boston Tea Party.

This is the harbor stained dark brown. "Like a giant teapot!"
shouted the sailors scared by disguises worn by the patriots
who made plans to dump the cargo
being carried in ships to the shores
of the colonists who cried, "No!"
to the king on his English throne who declared,
"Tax the tea!" that was made from the leaves
that grew on a bush in a far-off land
and became part of the Boston Tea Party.

These are tea chests, 340 in number, which bobbed in the harbor
stained dark brown. "Like a giant teapot!"
shouted the sailors scared by disguises worn by the patriots
who made plans to dump the cargo
being carried in ships to the shores
of the colonists who cried, "No!"
to the king on his English throne who declared,
"Tax the tea!" that was made from the leaves
that grew on a bush in a far-off land
and became part of the Boston Tea Party.

These are the soldiers who fought for freedom
remembering the tea chests, 340 in number, which bobbed in the harbor
stained dark brown. "Like a giant teapot!"
shouted the sailors scared by disguises worn by the patriots
who made plans to dump the cargo
being carried in ships to the shores
of the colonists who cried, "No!"
to the king on his English throne who declared,
"Tax the tea!" that was made from the leaves
that grew on a bush in a far-off land
and became part of the Boston Tea Party.

The redcoats are coming!

We're ready for them.

These are Americans, independent and free,
who honor the soldiers who fought for freedom
remembering the tea chests, 340 in number, which bobbed in the harbor
stained dark brown. "Like a giant teapot!"
shouted the sailors scared by disguises worn by the patriots
who made plans to dump the cargo
being carried in ships to the shores
of the colonists who cried, "No!"
to the king on his English throne who declared,
"Tax the tea!" that was made from the leaves
that grew on a bush in a far-off land
and became part of THE BOSTON TEA PARTY.

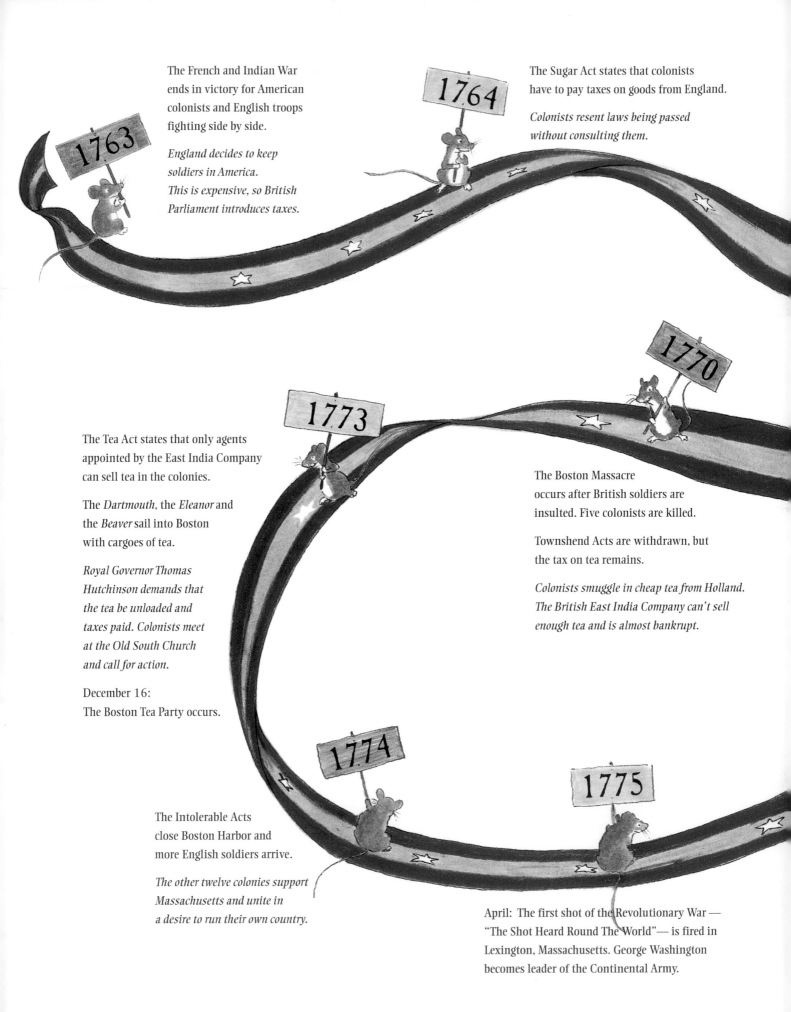

The French and Indian War ends in victory for American colonists and English troops fighting side by side.

England decides to keep soldiers in America. This is expensive, so British Parliament introduces taxes.

The Sugar Act states that colonists have to pay taxes on goods from England.

Colonists resent laws being passed without consulting them.

The Tea Act states that only agents appointed by the East India Company can sell tea in the colonies.

The *Dartmouth*, the *Eleanor* and the *Beaver* sail into Boston with cargoes of tea.

Royal Governor Thomas Hutchinson demands that the tea be unloaded and taxes paid. Colonists meet at the Old South Church and call for action.

December 16:
The Boston Tea Party occurs.

The Boston Massacre occurs after British soldiers are insulted. Five colonists are killed.

Townshend Acts are withdrawn, but the tax on tea remains.

Colonists smuggle in cheap tea from Holland. The British East India Company can't sell enough tea and is almost bankrupt.

The Intolerable Acts close Boston Harbor and more English soldiers arrive.

The other twelve colonies support Massachusetts and unite in a desire to run their own country.

April: The first shot of the Revolutionary War — "The Shot Heard Round The World" — is fired in Lexington, Massachusetts. George Washington becomes leader of the Continental Army.

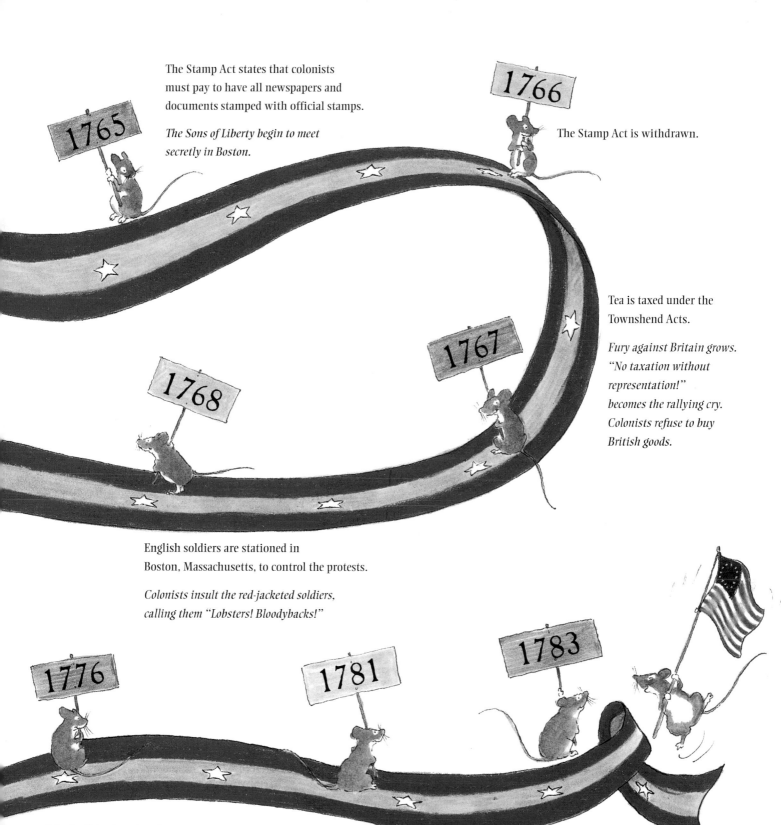

The Stamp Act states that colonists must pay to have all newspapers and documents stamped with official stamps.

The Sons of Liberty begin to meet secretly in Boston.

The Stamp Act is withdrawn.

Tea is taxed under the Townshend Acts.

Fury against Britain grows. "No taxation without representation!" becomes the rallying cry. Colonists refuse to buy British goods.

English soldiers are stationed in Boston, Massachusetts, to control the protests.

Colonists insult the red-jacketed soldiers, calling them "Lobsters! Bloodybacks!"

July 4: Colonists sign the Declaration of Independence.

October 19: English army surrenders to General George Washington.

September 3: The Treaty of Paris is signed, ending the war and recognizing U.S. independence.